Book 1:
Shark School

With thanks to Paul Ebbs

A TEMPLAR BOOK

First published in the UK in 2013 by Templar Publishing,
an imprint of The Templar Company Limited,
Deepdene Lodge, Deepdene Avenue,
Dorking, Surrey, RH5 4AT, UK

www.templarco.co.uk

ISBN 978-1-84877-732-3

Printed and bound by CPI Group (UK) Ltd,
Croydon, CR0 4YY

Shark School

by DAVY OCEAN

Illustrated by Aaron Blecha

templar

Chapter 1

I'm having my favourite dream again –
the one where I'm about to be crowned
Greatest Underwater Wrestling Champion
Of The World, Ever. I swim up to the top
rope of the ring and prepare to launch.

"I think he's going for a dropflick!"
a jellyfish commentator shouts into

his microphone.

"There's no stopping this hammerhead shark tonight," adds his partner, a bright orange clownfish.

"Ha-rry! Ha-rry!" the crowd begin to chant.

One diving dropflick and the blue shark I'm fighting will be fish food and the underwater wrestling belt will be mine. I dive down from the rope and pin my opponent to the canvas.

"Ha-rry! Ha-rry!" The crowd's voices get louder and louder. And louder. And then too loud. Like they are shouting right in my ear.

"HARRY – GET OFF!"

I open my left eye and swivel it
round. The wrestling ring disappears
and I am in my bedroom. Next to my bed.
And Humphrey, my humming-fish alarm
clock, is pinned to the floor under me.

"Let me go!" he yells.

"All right, all right," I mutter,
swimming back into bed. "Why did you

have to wake me? I was having a really cool dream."

"Don't tell me, the one about the wrestling match?" Humphrey says grumpily.

"Yes."

"I hate that dream."

"Why?"

"I always end up getting hurt."

I open my right eye and glare at him. "Only because you try to wake me up."

Humphrey starts swimming round in circles above my head. "It's my job to wake you up – I'm your alarm clock, and you've got school."

I groan. From almost being crowned Underwater Wrestling Champion Of The World to having to get ready for school, in less than ten seconds.

"So, are you awake then?"

"Yes!"

"Cool. See you tomorrow."

"Can't wait."

Humphrey swims off out of the window to go and get his breakfast.

I swivel my right eye around until I can see the huge poster of Gregor the Gnasher hanging on the rocky wall at the end of my bed. Gregor the Gnasher is the *actual* Underwater Wrestling Champion

of the World. In the poster, he's holding his winner's belt high above his head and smiling so widely you can see all of his three thousand and seventeen teeth. Gregor is a great white shark and as well as his rows and rows of razor-sharp teeth he has a long pointed snout and a humongous body. He's exactly what a shark *should* look like. And he's scary. Super scary. Even my poster of him makes my pet catfish poop itself.

If they made a poster of me, my catfish would probably just laugh. You see, I'm a hammerhead shark, which, for those of you who haven't already

worked it out,
means I have
a head that's
the shape of a
hammer. With
goggly eyes
so far apart
they look like
they've fallen
out with each
other. It's not

a great look. Especially if you want to be
taken seriously in the shark world.

I once made a list of the five coolest
sharks in existence. It went like this:

1. The great white – obviously.

2. The blue shark –
the fastest fish in
the sea.

3. The tiger shark –
scary and stripy.

4. The whale shark –
its mouth is so huge
it can swallow a
dolphin in one go!

ROAR.

5. The bull shark –
it can swim in
rivers as well as
the sea, which is
very handy if you're
going on holiday and stuff.

8

You may have noticed that the hammerhead shark isn't on the list. That's because the hammerhead shark is seriously uncool. In fact, the only shark less cool than a hammerhead is the nurse shark. Nurse sharks are the girliest sharks in the ocean – which is fine if you're a girl and everything, but I'm not.

Gregor doesn't just look cool, he can do loads of cool stuff too. Then I have a brainwave. I might not look like Gregor, but that doesn't mean I can't *be* like him. I swim out of bed and over to the old treasure chest where I keep my collection

of shells shaped like famous sportstars
and all of my lists. I once made a list of
all the cool stuff Gregor can do.
I take it out and study it.

Number one is out, obviously.

1. Wrestling – he's the Underwater
   Champion ten years running.

2. Eating boats – which scares the life
   out of the leggy air-breathers.

3. Looking really mean – without
   even trying.

4. Swimming fast – as fast
   as any speed-boat.

5. Ambushing prey – they
   never see him coming.

You can't just be Underwater Wrestling Champion Of The World in, like, two weeks or something. It takes years of deep-sea training: weight-lifting anchors, eating high-energy seaweed bars and swimming laps around ocean-liners.

Number two is a no-no as well. First of all, my mouth is way too small. Sometimes I find it hard swallowing a crab. Also, I'm not allowed up to the surface without one of my parents being with me. I know that sounds really lame – I mean, I'm ten years old. What do they think I'm going to do? Go for a sunbathe on the beach? And I'm not going to eat

any strange food dangling from fishing lines, either. Everyone knows what fishermen do to sharks when they catch them. They make their fins into soup, that's what. And there's no way I'd risk losing my fins. Imagine what a laughing stock I'd be then, with a head like a hammer and a body like an eel!

I put on my school tie and blazer and then read number three on my list. *Looking really mean.* Hmmm, now that sounds a bit easier. And if I looked really mean, certain sharks might not make fun of me any more. I swim over to my mirror and scrunch my eyes shut. Then I pull

my meanest face. I imagine I'm giving
the sort of fearsome scowl that Gregor
pulls when he's entering the wrestling
ring. It feels pretty good. I can already
imagine Rick Reef and his stupid sidekick
Donny Dogfish taking one look at the new
me and speeding off to hide behind the
school canteen.

But when I open my eyes and look in
the mirror, I don't see the mean monster
of my dreams – and
Rick Reef's nightmares
– I see a school kid who
looks like he's having
trouble doing a poo!

I swim back to the list feeling a bit worried. I'm starting to run out of options. Okay, number four. *Swimming fast.* I'm not bad at this, actually, but I'm not stupid – I'm never going to be as fast as Gregor. I look at number five. *Ambushing prey.* Aha – now surely I can do that. I mean, how hard can it be? I scan my bedroom looking for a victim. My eyes come to rest upon Larry, my lantern fish, snoozing away above my desk, his antennae glowing softly in the dark. Being careful not to make a sound, I start to glide through the water, Gregor's scary theme tune playing in my head.

DERRRRRRRRR-DUN!
DERRRRRRRR-DUN! DER-DUN! DER-
DUN! DER-DUN! DER-DUN!

But just as I get to the desk,
disaster strikes. My tail gets caught in
a strand from my seaweed blanket. I
try to tug it free but end up getting even
more tangled. I pull as hard as I can.
The balled-up blanket sails through the
water, hits the shelf above my bed and
sends my finball trophy flying.

"Eh? Uh! Wass going on?" Larry
says sleepily as I try to untangle myself
from the seaweed.

Hmm, not exactly the kind of

surprise attack I'd been planning. But the problem is, my room's way too small. You can't really sneak up on something when it's really close to start off with. You need a bit of distance from the target to be able to plan your attack. I decide to investigate the rest of the house to see what I can find.

But as I swim through my bedroom door, I hear a really horrible noise. It's like a crab grinding glass with its pincers. Or a ship's foghorn that has a seagull stuck inside it. It can only be one thing – my mum, singing while she makes the breakfast. I start to grin. When Mum is singing she goes off into her own little world and doesn't notice a thing. She will make the perfect target. Let the ambushing begin!

While Mum carries on screeching like a harpooned mermaid I get to the kitchen door without being seen. Then I poke one side of my hammerhead through the door and swivel my eye around, trying to spot my prey. There she is, at the far end of the kitchen, putting breakfast things on a tray, still singing away. Now I'm closer I can actually make out some of the words in between the screeches:

"Like an anchor – dropped for the very first time. Like an a-a-a-anchor..."

Oh please!

I slink my way into the room and slide behind the giant glass vase of flower fish in the corner. Honestly, I don't know why we can't just have proper sea flowers like everyone else. It was my

COVE SWEET COVE

dad's idea of a joke. But the trouble is, my dad's idea of a joke isn't ever anybody else's idea of a joke. I don't know how he managed to get elected as the new Shark Point mayor.

I get myself ready to pounce. This must be how Gregor feels before a fight, I think to myself as my heart starts to pound.

I hear my unsuspecting prey swimming for the door, her apron strings swishing in the water behind her. Closer and closer she comes.

"Made of iron, shiny and fine," she wails.

I tense my muscles. Closer she comes. I arch my back. And closer. I get ready to pounce. Closer. NOW!

Chapter 2

Okay, I'll admit it, the ambush didn't go one hundred per cent according to plan. It went about ten per cent according to plan. The surprise bit worked great – that was the ten per cent – but what happened straight after wasn't so brilliant. The chain of events went like this:

1. I leaped out from behind the flower fish, yelling at the top of my voice...

2. Mum screeched – and this time she wasn't singing...

3. Mum dropped the breakfast tray...

4. I smashed into it...

5. And sent everything flying EVERYWHERE.

And now everything has gone dark on one side of the room. I swivel my right eye but can't see anything out of it. My ambush has turned into a terrible tragedy!

"I'm blind! I'm blind!" I cry.

Mum stops screaming. "Breakfast bowl," she gasps, pointing a shaking fin at me.

I blink my working eye at her in disbelief. Why is she calling me breakfast bowl? Has my ambush made her go crazy? And why isn't she looking more concerned? Her only son has just told her he can't see any more! From one eye at least.

"What?" I say.

"Breakfast bowl."

"Why do you keep calling me that?" I yell. "I've gone blind in one eye."

"It's a breakfast bowl," she squeals.

"What are you talking about?" I start to panic. I have gone blind and my mum has gone crazy. So far this is not turning out to be a very good morning.

"You've got a breakfast bowl over your eye," mum explains.

I shake my head and, sure enough, a bowl falls off and drifts to the floor, leaving a splattering of kelp krispies trickling down my face. Although I'm relieved I'm not actually blind and my mum isn't actually crazy, I can't help thinking sadly that this would never, ever happen to Gregor the Gnasher.

"What in the name of all the oceans were you doing, Harry?" Mum asks.

"Sorry, Mum," I reply, looking at the floor. "I was only trying to ambush you."

"Only trying to ambush me!" Mum echoes, wiping the kelp krispies off my head with the bottom of her apron. (I bet that's never happened to Gregor either!) "Hammerheads don't ambush things, you silly little starfish!"

I cringe with embarrassment.

How am I ever going to be taken as seriously as a great white when my mum calls me names like that? "I was trying to be like Gregor the Gnasher," I try to explain.

Mum sighs. "I'll never understand why you kids think that tooth-head is some kind of hero."

"Hero? Did someone say hero?" my dad booms, entering the kitchen. "Well here I am! Ho, ho, ho!"

I told you his jokes weren't funny.

"Oh, you'll always be our hero, darling," laughs Mum, before giving him a massive kiss.

I think I might be sick. There's only so much a ten-year-old hammerhead can take in one morning.

"What was all that noise about?" Dad asks. He looks around at the mess. "And why's my breakfast on the floor?"

To stop Mum going through the whole ambush disaster again I decide to change the conversation.

"How's the speech going, Dad?"

My dad's working on his first ever speech as mayor. Most of Shark Point will be there to hear it so I hope he doesn't tell any jokes.

"It's going great," Dad replies, "but I think I should start with a joke. Better still, maybe two jokes..."

Where's a fisherman's hook when

you need one?

"How about this one?" says Dad as Mum sets about picking up the plates and bowls from the floor. "What do you call a fish with no eyes?"

I stare at him and shake my head. "I dunno."

"A fsh!" he replies before roaring with laughter. "Get it? No i's. Ho ho ho!"

He sees me staring at him, not laughing. "Okay, well, maybe I'll think of a different joke. I'll be in the living room." And with that he turns and swims back down the hall.

"Honey, can you turn on your

hammer-vision and see if you can find the lid for the teapot while I clear up?" Mum asks. "I must have dropped it in your... ambush."

I turn on the special sensors in my head and start swimming around the kitchen. Having sensors is a bit like having a load of extra eyes that can see inside and through things. And because our heads are so big, hammerheads have the most powerful sensors in the entire ocean. It's pretty cool. Especially if you want to find out where your parents have hidden your Christmas presents. Mum goes crazy when I do this. She says the reason we have sensors is so that we can find food even if it's buried deep beneath the seabed. She says that using our sensors to find hidden presents is wrong. But then she would say that – she's a parent. As far as parents are concerned, everything that's good fun is 'wrong'!

I find the teapot lid straightaway –
behind a sea cucumber on the table.

"Thank you, dear," Mum says as
I give it to her. "You've certainly got
excellent hammer-vision – and it's so
much more useful than ambushing.
I mean, who needs to hunt for prey these
days, when you can just pop down to the
shops?"

"But ambushing's exciting and
cool," I reply. "When I use my sensors I'm
just... trying to find stuff."

"What is cool," says Mum, "is your
class outing to the Titan today. So you'd
better get some breakfast inside you or

you're going to be late."

The Titan! I'd completely forgotten about the school trip to the shipwreck. It wasn't as exciting as going out to the deep ocean to see great whites – but it was a day out of school.

I barely manage to cram down some breakfast before I hear Ralph shouting for me outside. Ralph is a pilot fish and one of my best friends.

I grab my backpack and head for the door.

"Bye, Mum. Bye, Dad."

"Bye, angel-fish!" Mum calls.

"Bye, son," Dad hollers. "What kind

of fish feels the most pain?"

I pretend not to hear him.

"A sore-dine! Ho ho ho!"

My parents are so embarrassing!

Outside, Ralph is swimming around our front garden, his silver stripes glinting in the sunshine.

"Hey, Harry, all set for the school trip?" he says as soon as he sees me.

"You bet," I reply.

"So what did you have for breakfast today?" he asks.

"Shrimp Pop-Tarts."

"Cool, my favourite. Okay then, open wide, I'm going in!"

I open my mouth as wide as I can and Ralph dives in and starts nibbling at my teeth.

This is what pilot fish do by the way – they eat the scraps of food from between sharks' teeth. They're kind of like swimming, talking toothbrushes.

As soon as Ralph has finished we start making our way towards the centre of town.

We've just reached the water park when Joe turns up. Joe is a bright yellow jellyfish and another one of my friends. One of the most cool things about Joe is that he has quite a few arms. Well, *a lot* of arms. The only uncool thing about Joe's arms is that it can take a *long* time to high-five. I like him a lot, but he can be a bit of a worrier.

"Good morning, Joe," I say.

"Is it?" Joe replies.

Ralph and I stare at him.

36

"Of course it is – we're going on the trip to the Titan," says Ralph.

"Aren't you looking forward to it?" I ask.

"Not really," says Joe. "I'll probably get my tentacles trapped in a porthole, or be harpooned by a diver. Or lose my packed lunch in the wreckage, or—"

"Okay, okay, we get the point," says Ralph.

Joe's yellow tentacles quiver.

"Why can't we just stay in school?

It's much safer."

"Oh come on, Joe," I say. "It'll be good to see more of the ocean."

"Why?" he replies. "It's all the same – just a lot of wet."

You can't really argue with that, so we stop at the shops and look in Seahorse Sports and Leisure to check out the latest games. Then we make our way to school. My heart sinks as I see Rick Reef and Donny Dogfish by the gates. Rick is a blacktip reef shark, which means he has this really cool black tip on his dorsal fin. He is wearing his matching black leather jacket (as usual) and showing off (as usual) by swimming really quickly through all the groups of kids. Donny is cheering him on (as usual), doing a sports commentary as Rick speeds about.

"And Rick Reef takes a sharp right past some Year Two clownfish and a left through a group of Year One dolphins. See them scatter as the swimming captain speeds down the straight."

Rick is the school swimming

captain and loves to let everyone know it.

Suddenly Rick spots our group and swims straight for us, pulling up at the last minute and showering us with air bubbles.

"Well, if it isn't old anchor face," he says.

"Good one, Rick," says Donny, smirking away beside him.

"Oh grow up, Rick," says Ralph.

"Shut up, Toothpick," says Rick. Then he turns to Joe. "Oh look, it's Jelly Belly."

Donny is almost killing himself laughing, but before anyone can say anything else the school bell rings.

"Last one in's a sea snail," shouts

Rick as he swims for the door.

I'll show him who's a sea snail, I think to myself as I charge after him.

"What are you doing?" Ralph cries.

"Be careful," Joe calls, "you might sprain your tail, or pull a fin muscle."

But I don't care. Nothing and no-one is going to stop me. I'm going to teach that reef shark show-off a lesson. He might be the fastest swimmer in the school but I have surprise on my side. Rick thinks no-one would actually bother racing him because he's the swimming captain, so he isn't going that fast. I zoom past him into the school.

I speed along the corridor. The classroom door is getting closer all the time. I swivel my left eye backwards and see that Rick's gaining on me.

DERRRRRRRRR-DUN! DERRRRRRRR-DUN! DER-DUN! DER-DUN! DER-DUN! DER-DUN!

I think of Gregor the Gnasher's theme tune and make a desperate lunge for the door.

DERRRRRRRRR-DUN! DERRRRRRRR-DUN! DER—

"Ow!"

I'm so busy keeping one eye on Rick I forget that the doorway is kind of

narrow and go slamming straight into it.
I desperately flail my tail but it's no good.
I'm stuck, my humongous hammerhead
wedged in the door.

"Hey, Harry," I hear Rick tease
from behind me, chuckling, "I've heard
of getting something in your eye – but a

whole door frame?"

The entire class start laughing their heads off. And they are still laughing as Ralph and Joe help me unwedge myself. I've never felt more embarrassed as I slink over to my desk.

But it had felt so good when I was

actually beating Rick in the race. I decide there and then that I don't care what it takes, I'm going to prove I'm just as good as the rest of them. I'm going to show them all what a hammerhead can do!

Chapter 3

Creeeeeeeeeeeeeeeeeeeaaaaaaaaaaaaak!!!

At first I think the noise is coming from the rotting timbers of the Titan.

Creeeeeeeeeeeeee-ak-ak-ak-ak-ak!!!

But it isn't the Titan.

It's Joe's bum.

Me and Ralph give him a look.

"Well, it is a bit scary!" Joe says, turning from bright yellow to bright pink with embarrassment.

And to be honest, Joe is spot on. It *is* scary.

As Mrs Shelby, our sea-turtle teacher, leads us closer to the Titan, the butterflies start to flap in my tummy

too. The wreck looms out of the green deep-sea gloom, dripping with seaweed and rust. The dark portholes along the side are like rows of spooky eyes staring at us. They make me want to shiver. But I'm not going to show that I'm scared, not with Rick and Donny hanging at the back of the line chewing sea-gum and blowing bubbles into rude shapes. And besides, Gregor the Gnasher wouldn't be scared of an old shipwreck. No way.

Mrs Shelby brings us to a halt beneath the enormous prow of the Titan. It towers over us like a cliff.

"Now class," Mrs Shelby says,

peering over her little round glasses. The shadow from the shipwreck has made her brown face go really dark. "Under no circumstances are you to go into the wreck. It is very, very dangerous in there. The Titan has been on the seabed for over a hundred years, and is rusting and rotting away. It could collapse at any moment and turn you into fish paste!"

Everyone giggles, until we see the serious look on Mrs Shelby's face.

"I mean it. You're here to look at the area around the Titan for your geography project." Mrs Shelby begins handing round flat pieces of rock with writing on.

"Here is a list of everything I want you to find."

Now normally I love lists, but not this one.

1.   A barnacle – boring!

2.   Three different types of shell – more boring!

3.   At least three colours of seaweed – I'm seriously starting to fall asleep now.

4.   Zzzzzzzzzzzzzzzzzzzzzzzzzz – see.

Ralph fins me in the side to wake me up.

"Once you've found everything on your checklist, meet back here, under the prow, okay?" Mrs Shelby calls.

We all nod and start to swish away.

"Wait!"

We all stop.

"I need to put you in your groups."

Mrs Shelby has a thing about us working in groups. It's really annoying. Doesn't she realise that I'm a shark, a lone hunter of the waves? I bet Gregor never gets put in a group. When she first starts reading the names of my group it isn't too bad.

1.   Joe – Yay!
2.   Ralph – Double Yay!
3.   Me – Hooray!
4.   Donny – Boooooo!
5.   Rick – Double Boooooo! with extra Boooooo! on the side and sprinkled with grated Boooooo!

"Now don't forget what I told you," Mrs Shelby yells as we start to swim off. "No going inside the Titan – UNDER ANY CIRCUMSTANCES!"

"Yes, Mrs Shelby," we all mutter.

Of course Rick straightaway takes the lead in our group and decides which way we swim. We all follow him round to the collapsed stern of the Titan. It must have hit the seabed with a massive crunch. The whole back of the ship with its four enormous propellers is ripped open and we can see right inside. The decks are layered like Mum's coral-cake, and great tumbles of stuff like bed frames and chairs and doors and ladders have all fallen out onto the seabed in a big fan-shaped mess. It's starting to get covered in seaweed and barnacles and coral – it won't be long before the whole thing turns into a new reef. And Rick is leading us straight into it!

I look around, but can only see the back of Mrs Shelby's shell as she comforts Penny Puffer-Fish. Penny has gone all spiky. Puffer-fish only get spiky when they are very afraid and think they are about to die. Penny must be *very* scared of the Titan.

"Rick!" I call as loud as I dare.

"You heard what Mrs Shelby said."

Rick looks back, smirks and says, "I thought you were a hammerhead, not a scaredy-cat-fish. Me and Donny are going into the wreck, coz that's where all the best barnacles are, and we're going to have the best project. Are you coming, or are you going to stay there making bubbles with your bums?"

Donny and Rick slap fins and swoosh off, right towards the hole in the back of the Titan.

Well, I'm not going to stand for that. "Come on guys, let's go!" I cry.

"Where?" Ralph and Joe say together.

"With them," I shout, pointing after Rick and Donny. I can see that Ralph isn't sure, and Joe is actually trying to hide under himself.

"It'll be fine," I say.

"Yeah, if FINE stands for 'we'll be **F**ishfood, **I**f **N**ot **E**xterminated'," Joe mutters from beneath his tentacles.

With a bit of pushing and pulling, me, Ralph and, finally, Joe head off towards the wreck.

Rick and Donny have already disappeared by the time we get to the massive hole in the back of the ship. Jagged strips of metal hang above us as sharp as razor-shells. Thick, water-logged beams of wood ripped from floors and walls look splintery and deadly.

"It feels colder. Does it feel colder to you?" Joe says with a shiver. "I'm turning from a jellyfish into a lollyfish. I'm going to freeze and die. I've already lost the feeling in my seventh tentacle!"

Ralph swims up to me with a barnacle in his fins. "Got one let's go," he says with a tremble in his voice.

I'm just about to agree when some stuff happens. Stuff that means I'm not leaving the wreck. Well, not yet.

The stuff that happens is:

1. Rick appears with a big, toothy grin.
2. Donny arrives back too (but he doesn't look as grinny. In fact, he looks a bit bottom-poppy).
3. Rick **flubbers** the side of my hammer with his fin.

4.   **Flubbering** the side of my hammer
      with his fin makes my stupid rubbery head
      boing about and makes my words come out
      all **flibbery**.

5.   "D-d-d-d-d-d-don't
      d-d-d-d-d-d-d-do
      d-d-d-d-d-d-dat!"
      See?

Luckily Ralph and Joe know what
to do. They each catch an end of my head
and hold on tightly until it stops *flibber-*
flabbering.

      "Come on, Rubberhead," Rick says,
"look what we've found!"

      I hate it when Rick flubbers my head.

Hammerheads are the only sharks you can do it to, and he does it all the time. It makes me feel stupid. Well, I'm not going to let him see me scared too!

With one kick of my tail, I follow, and as Ralph and Joe are still holding onto my head, they come too.

As I swim on into the Titan it gets darker and darker. I'm not really taking much notice of what's around me – I'm just determined to keep up with Rick and Donny. I can hear Ralph and Joe making muffled cries as they hug onto my head, but I'm not stopping for anything.

Then!

Wow!

We have come out into a huge ballroom right in the middle of the Titan. The whole place is lit up but I don't understand why. Then I look up to the ceiling. There's a hole in it and sunlight from the ocean surface is pouring in. I can see more collapsed decks above it

leading up to massive ships' funnels,
bent over at crazy angles. They look
like they've been caught in mid-fall by
invisible hands. It looks really spooky!
Although the middle of the ballroom is
quite bright from the sun, the edges are
covered in really dark shadow. Anything
could be hiding there, waiting to pounce...

Rick starts swimming around the ballroom, darting in and out of the seaweed-covered pillars. Then he starts doing barrel rolls and fin slides. He tail-flips into a double nosey and skims underneath me with a triple gill slap.

Show-off, I think to myself.

"How cool is this place, and how cool am I?" shouts Rick as he shoots off again.

That's the final straw. It's time I show this show-off exactly what a hammerhead is capable of! Shaking Ralph and Joe clear, I speed off after Rick, knocking Donny right out of the way as I do.

Rick skids into a full tailspin. I give him my best double gill flip. Rick just laughs in my face and is off again, tail-grinding along a handrail and single-finning across the gap between two torn-open rooms.

I follow. And then I make several mistakes, so many I can make a list of them.

1.   I follow Rick without thinking – bad.

2.   Not thinking means I don't measure the gap he goes through – bad, bad.

3.   Not measuring the gap he goes through means I crash into the ragged gap in a half-twisty double-fin with pike – bad, bad, bad.

4. And I was probably travelling at twice my normal speed – bad beyond belief.

Creeeeeeeeeaaaaaaaaaaaakkkk!!!!

"That wasn't my bum!" I hear Joe shouting as I thud into the wall with a huge... thud.

I have just enough time to look up before the half-collapsed funnels above the ballroom start falling towards us with a horrible crashing, smashing, tearing, ripping sound.

And then everything goes dark!

Chapter 4

I think what happens next is this:

1. Donny crashes into Rick.

2. Rick crashes into me.

3. I crash into Joe.

4. Two of Joe's tentacles get stuck in my nostrils and I have to shake my head like crazy until my slimy jellyfish mate lets go.

The funnel has crashed down over the hole in the ballroom ceiling and nearly all the light has gone. I try to keep calm, but it's not easy. Especially when you've had jellyfish fingers stuck up your nose. But now Joe has finally let go I'm finding it easier to breathe. And I might not be able to see much but I can still *hear* stuff.

I can hear someone's teeth chattering.

"Is everyone okay?" I ask.

"I want my mummy," says Joe.

"Me too!" says Donny.

"M-m-m-e-e thr-r-e-e-e," says someone else.

"Ralph? Is that you?" I ask.

"N-n-n-n-no," says Rick, "It-it-it-it's me."

I'm shocked. Big, brave Rick the reef shark is so scared he can't keep his teeth still!

"W-w-w-what happened?" Rick asks.

"The funnel fell down," I say.

"We need to get out of here!" yells Donny. "It's not safe! We'll be crushed!"

"He's r-r-r-r-right!" Rick says.

"Wait!" I start to say, but Donny is off. I feel him skim past me.

"No!" Donny calls back, "I'm going back out the way we—"

BOINNNNNNNNNNNG...
CREEEEEEEEEEEEEEEEEEEEEEEEAK...

CRASH!

I think these noises are:

1. Donny going BOINNNNNNNNNNG as he bounces off a big metal door that has blocked the way we came in.

2. The vibration of the BOINNNNNNNNNNG causing the funnel to CREEEEEEEEEEEEE EEEEEEEEEEEEEEEEAK again.

3. The CREEEEEEEEEEEEEEEEEEEEEAK of the funnel causing a load of timbers from the ceiling to CRASH down. Only just missing me, Joe and Rick!

"Nobody move!" I shout. "We can't see anything, and every time we knock into something we make things even worse."

"W-w-w-why are y-y-y-y-you s-s-s-suddenly in ch-ch-ch-ch-charge?" Rick chatters.

"Because my mouth isn't doing stupid things with my teeth," I say.

"I-I-I-I-I-I'm j-j-j-just c-c-c-c-cold," Rick whines. "That's all."

Yeah right, I think. But I don't say anything because I have more important things to think about. Like where's Ralph?

"Where's Ralph?" I ask.

Silence.

"Ralph! Ralph!" I shout.

"He's probably dead," Joe says gloomily. "I told you we'd be fish food if

72

we came in here."

Silence.

POP.

"Joe!" Donny yells.

"Sorry," Joe mutters.

I swim about a bit, slowly and carefully. "Ralph? Are you okay?" But there's no sound apart from—

CREEEEEEEEEEEEEEEEEAK

The timbers and the funnel shift again. But this time with no-one bumping into anything. This is getting serious. We're trapped in a collapsing ship and

I can't find my best friend! I clamp my jaw shut to stop *my* teeth chattering with fear. I have to at least pretend to be brave or we'll never make it out.

"Okay, listen up everyone, we've got to find Ralph and then we can get out of here."

"He's your f-f-f-friend, you f-f-f-find him!" says Rick. Donny just looks away.

I'm not going to get any help from the Terrified Twins, that's for sure.

I turn to look at Joe. He's wobbling his tentacles about in panic, mumbling, "**F**ishfood, **I**f **N**ot **E**xterminated. Why doesn't anyone ever listen to me?"

I'm beginning to wish I *had* listened to him.

There's nothing else for it. I gulp and try not to look scared. "Right, you all stay here and I'll go and look for Ralph."

I kick my tail and swim off cautiously. My goggly eyes are a bit more used to the dark now and I can start to make out some shapes. Lots of the ballroom's ceiling has come down all around us, but the huge, rusty funnel is lying right across the hole. You couldn't even fit a flatfish through the gap now. We are well and truly trapped.

I start to swim around in a circle,

looking up and down, hoping that Ralph hasn't been hit by any of the falling wood. My heart is beating so hard I can feel it shaking my whole body.

From the other side of the ballroom Joe starts muttering again. "I reckon we're going to be stuck here so long we won't be home for tea."

I swim alongside a pile of crushed chairs.

"In fact, we'll probably freeze to death before we ever get out."

I dart over broken, seaweed-covered tables.

"The only way I'm getting out of

here is if some whale crashes his way in
and fancies a jellyfish ice-lolly."

I stick my head into a slimy
fireplace. Still no Ralph.

"Or we'll get crushed up into
plankton and eaten. Everyone'll wonder
where we've got to. They'll probably run
a missing fishes advert in the *Seaweed
Times*, but it'll be too late. I just know
we're not going to get out! I can sense it."

I'm just about to tell Joe to shut up,
when something hits me like a wet fish in
the face.

Sense it!

Joe said he could 'sense it'.

Oh flibbery-flump! Of course. I can use my sensors to try and find Ralph. I quickly turn them on and start moving my hammerhead about, scanning the room. It's really faint, but I can definitely sense some movement coming from the other end of the ballroom. I swim off past Joe and I zoom in on the tiny vibration I can sense in my hammer.

BRRRRRMMMMMM

As I reach the far end of the
ballroom, the vibration gets much
stronger. It's not clear exactly where
the vibration is coming from, but it's
definitely around here somewhere.

I look left.

BRRRRrrrrrrrrmmmmmmmmm...

I look right.

...mmmmMMMMBBBBRRRRRR!!!

I go right, and find a big pile of timbers. Underneath the timbers is a grand piano – one of those that has a big lid on top. It's standing all lopsided on broken legs. The lid is shut, and covered in pieces of the fallen ceiling. But what I see sticking out from the lid makes my hammerhead quiver. Waving slowly in the tiny gap is the bottom half of Ralph.

He's trapped inside the piano!

"Ralph! Ralph! It's me!" I shout.

"Harry?" Ralph squeaks from inside the piano, "Help! I can't move."

I rush forward and try and push the piano lid up with my fin.

It won't budge.

I flip around and shove my tail up against the pile of wood on top. I push as hard as I can.

It won't budge either.

"Or maybe we'll get captured by leggy air-breathers, who are doing research on the shipwreck, and no-one will ever see us again," I hear Joe muttering from the other side of the room.

81

I take three swishes of my tail backwards, turn and face the piano head on, and leap towards it hammer-first. It hurts but I manage to get the flat edge of my head into the gap beneath the piano lid.

I flick my tail harder and the lid creaks up a tiny bit, giving me enough room to slide my eye into the crack. I can see Ralph. He's on his side and still stuck, but he looks okay.

"Don't worry, Ralph," I say, "I'll soon have you out of here."

I can feel the weight of the timbers on the piano lid pressing on to my head,

but I don't care, I've got to get Ralph out.
But how? Maybe if I twisted my head
sideways I'd be able to lift the lid higher.

I start kicking really hard with my
tail fin.

The lid moves up a bit.

I kick a bit harder.

It moves up a bit more.

I flap and flip my tail as hard as I
can and twist my head until—

The lid springs up, tumbling the
timbers onto the floor.

Ralph speeds out of the piano faster
than a sailfish. I'm right behind him.

"Yaaaaaaaaaaaaaaaaaaaaaaaaaaaa

aaaaaay!" we both scream, high-finning each other and bumping chests.

"I thought I was never going to get out of there," Ralph gasps. "What happened?"

"Part of the ceiling caved in," I explain as we swim back over to the others. "And a funnel came down and blocked the hole."

We swim over to Joe, who is still sat on the floor hiding behind his tentacles.

"Look – I found Ralph!" I say.

Joe moves one of his tentacles and peeps out. But when he sees Ralph he doesn't look happy.

"What's wrong?" I say.

"We're still done for. Even if nothing happens to us, we'll still starve to death." Joe puts his tentacle back over his eyes.

Ralph and I roll *our* eyes. I look about and my heart sinks. "Where's Rick and Donny?"

"They said they weren't waiting for you to find Ralph and were going to smash their way out," Joe says.

CRAAAAAAAAAAAAAAAAAAAAAASH!!!!

"That'll be them then," says Joe.

Oh no!

I swim as fast as I can to the metal door. Rick and Donny are bashing themselves against it in panic. I try and swim between Rick and the door. "Stop it!" I yell. "You'll bring the whole ship down on us!"

But Donny noses me out of the way and Rick thuds into the door again.

There's nothing I can do to stop them.

"Look at the funnel!" Ralph yells.

I look up. The funnel is shifting again and the timbers holding it up are beginning to give way. If we don't get out of here soon we're fish cakes.

I dart back to Ralph and Joe. "Come on, let's try over there!" I point a fin to the far corner of the ballroom. Then I call back to Rick and Donny. "Come on you two."

"You go if you w-w-w-want to," Rick shouts at me. "But we're not moving. This is the way w-w-w-w-we came in and this is the way we're going out. That way will just take you further into the ship and

you'll be even more trapped."

I don't want to leave them, but if there's another way out I *have* to find it.

Joe, Ralph and I swim along the wall, until we reach a jumbled pile of rotting furniture. We swim higher and higher up the pile, until, right at the top, we find a big sofa with springs popping out all over it, like a puffer fish gone spiky.

"Careful," I say to the other two as I dodge the springs. Once we've got past the pyramid of furniture I can't believe my goggly eyes. There's a door! And it doesn't seem to be blocked by anything. "Let's see where it goes," I call to the other two. "If it leads out of the ship we can go and get Donny and Rick."

It's even colder on the other side of the doorway. We swim down a short, dark corridor, which opens on to a massive landing and a huge broken staircase as wide as a whale sandwich.

"Wow," I say.

Huge marble pillars have toppled down and smashed through the staircase. They look like a giant's fingers breaking through the wood.

Ralph and Joe start swimming around looking for a way out, but there is only the staircase which just seems to

lead up to nowhere.

"Looks like we're stuck," says Ralph.

"Trapped in a watery grave," says
Joe mournfully.

I swim to the bottom of the stairs

and squint through the waving strands of seaweed and murky water. Then I catch sight of something.

"Yes!" I cry.

Right up high, almost but not quite out of range of my hammerhead eyes, I can see a tiny glimmer of light. I swivel my eyes and focus them as hard as I can. There, high above us, in the roof of the Titan, is a skylight. It's been smashed and through it I can see a beam of sunlight in the water.

It's a way out!

We're saved!

Or we would have been. But that's

when the whole ship begins to shake and rumble, and the hugest **CRASH!!!** yet comes from the direction of the ballroom.

Chapter 5

Me, Ralph and Joe burst back into the ballroom and find the water churning up like a whirlpool, full of dust and bits of wood.

"Rick!" I call. "Donny! Are you okay?" But there's no answer. "Split up," I say to Ralph and Joe. "We've got to find them and get up those stairs."

"Okay," Ralph says.

Joe is fishing bits of dirt out of his mouth with his tentacles. "Mmmph mmmph we'll be exploded into jelly beans mmmph," he says.

"Come on!" I say.

We all swim off in different directions. I head for the metal door, and just when I think the day can't get any worse, it does.

Donny is swimming in circles by the door, crying and shaking.

"Where's Rick?" I say.

Donny points a trembling fin

behind me.

I turn and squint through the murky water. And see Rick trapped inside a glittery gold cage. I can hardly believe my eyes. So I blink them. Then I swivel them. But I wasn't seeing things – Rick really is trapped inside a glittery gold cage.

What I think happened is this:

1.　　Donny and Rick kept smashing into the door. (Not good.)

2.　　The vibrations they caused travelled up through the ship until they reached the ceiling. (Not gooder.)

3.　　This shook one of the enormous chandeliers so much that it crashed down on top of Rick and trapped him to the floor. (Not gooder-er!)

"Get me out," Rick wails.

RUUUUUUUUUUMMMMMBLE

The whole ship vibrates. Clouds of splinters puff out from the joists above us like coral blooms. The ballroom is about to collapse completely. Ralph and Joe swim over in panic.

"Don't just float there! Get me out!" Rick yells.

Donny is still swimming round and round in circles. I grab him by the fins. "Donny! We need your help. We won't be able to get Rick out on our own."

Donny's eyes are filled with tears and his bottom lip is trembling. "You don't even like Rick so why would you want to help him?"

"Well, I wouldn't leave him here to get crushed, would I?"

Donny sniffs. "I suppose not."

"Good, now are you going to help us or what?"

Donny nods, and I pat him on the fin.

"Get me out!" Rick screams.

"Right," I say, trying to sound like
I know what I'm doing and I have a plan,
which I don't. "Ummmm..."

The chandelier is massive. The
gold rails are all bent over in arches.

There are loads
of little hoops
attached, which
were probably
used for glass
baubles or
something, but
now they're just

empty. These hoops are what I'm *really* interested in.

Now I have a plan!

"Okay, everyone wedge your fin into a hoop on this side of the chandelier," I say.

No one moves.

Joe opens his mouth to speak, but I cut him off.

"No, we're not going to freeze to death, or become ice-lollies and eaten by whales, or get turned into plankton, or get featured in the *Seaweed Times*, or captured by leggy air-breathers, or starve to death, or exploded into jelly beans. At least we won't if you *hurry up*!" I say.

"No, it's not that," Joe says.

"What is it then?" I ask.

"GET ME OUT!" Rick yells.

"What if you haven't got a fin?" Joe asks.

"Oh! Well, use your strongest tentacles," I say.

RUUUUUUUUUUMMMMMBLE

"Now!" I shout. "We haven't got time to be scared!"

I wriggle my right fin up into a hoop and shove my dorsal fin against it. The others do the same but I can see the fear in their faces as they all look over to me to show that they're ready.

This had better work.

"Rick – get ready to swim out, okay?" I say.

"Just hurry up!" Rick yells.

"Okay everyone," I shout. "Swim up now!"

I kick with my tail. Ralph and Donny do the same. Joe does something complicated with his tentacles.

The chandelier shifts a tiny bit, but not enough!

"Get me out!"

CRRRRREEEEEEEEAAAAAKKKKKK!!!!!!

This is our last chance!

"One. Two..." I count.

Joe's bottom pops.

"Three!"

I kick and kick and kick my tail, harder than I've ever done before.

The chandelier starts to move.

"Keep going!" I shout.

Kick.

Kick.

Kick. Kick. Kick!

The chandelier lurches upwards. Rick flattens himself against the floor, and slides underneath the edges of the cage. He's out!

"Okay, let go," I yell.

We all swim away and the

chandelier crashes back to the floor.

"Follow me," I say, swimming for the doorway leading to the staircase. We zoom across the decking, up over the pile of wrecked furniture, past the springs of the busted sofa, and out through the door into the dark corridor. I can hear the others flapping behind me. I turn to make sure everyone is through the door okay. Rick, Donny, Ralph and then Joe, puffing up behind. Jellyfish aren't exactly built for speed but he's doing a brilliant job.

"Right, everyone, up the stairs. Up to the skylight. Come on!"

We race up the stairs towards the skylight and burst out of the roof like corks from a bottle, whooping and high-finning each other like crazy. Down below us there is a final **RUUUUUUUUUUMMMMMMBLE** as the

Titan collapses like a seashell being
squashed by a giant fin!

Chapter 6

I don't think I've ever seen Mrs
Shelby look so happy. She's smiling wide
enough to swallow a baby whale.

"Harry! Ralph! Joe! Donny! Rick!"
she calls to us. "Oh my goodness, I've
been so worried!"

We swim down to the seabed,

where Mrs Shelby has gathered the class together out of danger. All the kids look pretty scared by the noises coming from the Titan. Not only is Penny Puffer-Fish still spiky but all the hermit crab kids have gone right inside their shells and shut the doors.

We skid to a halt in front of the class, me doing a triple nosey and the best gill grind ever.

"We thought you were trapped inside!" Mrs Shelby says, hugging each of us in turn. She probably hugs Joe just a little bit too tight because he pops again, but she doesn't seem to mind.

I'm just about to tell her everything
that happened when a fin slaps onto
my face and covers my mouth so I can't
speak. The fin belongs to Rick. He pushes
in front of me. "Well, Miss, if I hadn't got
everyone out, we might not have made it

at all. Right Donny?"

I stare so hard at Rick it feels like my eyes might pop out of my hammerhead. I can't believe what he's saying. Just a couple of minutes ago he was shrieking for help, stuck under a chandelier.

"I tried to tell them not to go in to the Titan, Miss, but they wouldn't listen," Rick continues. "And I couldn't just leave them to go in alone, could I?"

I glance at Ralph and Joe. They look just as annoyed as me. We're all so annoyed we can't get any words out!

This is so unfair. I start to open my mouth to complain but then all the kids in the class start laughing. Great! So now not only do they think I've got a stupid hammerhead, they think I'm a coward too. But as I swivel my eyes around I notice that the rest of the class are all pointing and laughing at Rick. As he swims about in front of Mrs Shelby I see something glinting and sparkling on his back. Some baubles from the chandelier have got caught on his dorsal fin like a princess's tiara.

He looks
ridiculous.

I begin
laughing too,
so hard I end
up doing three
barrel rolls. By
the time I finish,
Mrs Shelby is
waving her big flippers
to calm the class down and Rick is just
floating there with a bright red face.

"What are you all laughing at?" he
whines.

Ha! Now he knows what it feels like maybe he won't *flubber* my head so much in future. Win!

Ralph swims past me and turns to the class. "We wouldn't have got out of there if it wasn't for Harry, Miss," he says. "It was Rick who wanted to go into the Titan, not Harry. When the funnel collapsed and everything went dark, I got trapped inside a piano and it was Harry and his hammerhead sensors that got me out. Rick was too busy trying to save his own skin. Harry is the bravest shark in the whole sea."

I feel my hammerhead going coral

pink as the whole class looks from Rick's tiara to me. I don't really like being the centre of attention – even if it's for a good thing. But Ralph carries on. "And when Rick got trapped under a chandelier, it was Harry who showed us how to get him out, and it was Harry's brilliant hammerhead eyes that found the way out through the skylight. All Rick did while we were in there was show off and cry."

Everyone in the class is staring open-mouthed at me. Even Mrs Shelby. I don't know what to say.

Mrs Shelby closes her mouth,

thinks for a moment, then beckons me and Rick forward. "You two boys are very, very naughty for disobeying me and going into the Titan. If you'd listened to me none of this would have happened, and none of you would have been in any danger at all. Do you understand?"

We both nod. This makes Rick's tiara sparkle and the three angelfish behind us giggle under their breath.

"Really I should punish you all for going into the ship," Mrs Shelby continues, "but seeing as Harry has been so brave, and he managed to bring you all back to safety, I shall let you off. But just this once, mind!"

The class cheers and claps. Ralph and Joe swim up to me and we high-fin and high-tentacle.

Donny slopes off to one side with Rick, and I watch as he whispers in his ear, telling him about the tiara. Rick twists and turns his pointy face, trying to get a look at his fin.

"Get it off me!"

he yells at Donny.

Donny pulls at the baubles with his teeth and Rick twists some more. But the baubles are stuck fast and their struggles only make the class laugh even louder. Donny and Rick look like they are dancing together in that really embarrassing way that mums and dads do.

Mrs Shelby calms the class down all over again. Then we set off back to school. As we go I make my final list of the day – of all the good things that have happened:

1)   Everyone is safe. (Brilliant.)

2)   Rick's tiara incident is going to keep him

from picking on me for a bit. (Sparkly brilliant!)

3)   What started out as the worst day ever has turned into the best day ever! (More-sparkly-than-Rick's-tiara brilliant!)

Being a hammerhead might not be so bad after all...

THE END

HARRY

Species: hammerhead shark

You'll spot him... using his special hammervision

Favourite thing: his Gregor the Gnasher poster

Most likely to say: "I wish I was a great white."

Most embarrassing moment: when Mum called him her 'little starfish' in front of all his friends

RALPH

Species: pilot fish

You'll spot him... eating the food from between Harry's teeth!

Favourite thing: shrimp Pop-Tarts

Most likely to say: "So Harry, what's for breakfast today?"

Most embarrassing moment: eating too much cake on Joe's birthday. His face was COVERED in pink plankton icing.

JOE

Species: jellyfish

You'll spot him… hiding behind Ralph and Harry, or behind his own tentacles

Favourite thing: his cave, as it's nice and safe

Most likely to say: "If we do this, we're going to end up as fish food…"

Most embarrassing moment: whenever his bum goes POP, which is when he's scared. Which is all the time.

RICK

Species: blacktip reef shark

You'll spot him... bullying smaller fish or showing off

Favourite thing: his black leather jacket

Most likely to say: "Last one there's a sea snail!"

Most embarrassing moment: none. Rick's far too cool to get embarrassed.

Coming soon...

More funny fishy tales from Harry and the gang.

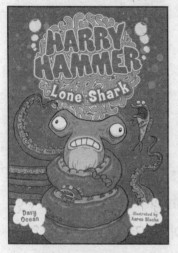

August 2013
ISBN: 978-1-84877-734-7

August 2013
ISBN: 978-1-84877-735-4

www.harry-hammer.co.uk

STINKY and JINKS

www.stinkyandjinks.blogspot.co.uk

Out now
ISBN: 978-1-84877-293-9

Out now
ISBN: 978-1-84877-294-6

July 2013
ISBN: 978-1-84877-295-3